Just Grace

CRINKLES

Me

BUG

Just Grace

Written and illustrated
by
Charise Mericle Harper

Houghton Mifflin Harcourt
Boston New York

www.hmhco.com

The text of this book is set in Dante.
The illustrations are pen-and-ink drawings digitally colored in Photoshop.

The Library of Congress has cataloged the hardcover edition as follows:
Harper, Charise Mericle.
Just Grace / written and illustrated by Charise Mericle Harper.
p. cm.
Summary: Misnamed by her teacher, seven-year-old Just Grace
prides herself on being empathetic, but when she tries to help a neighbor
feel better, her good intentions backfire.
[1. Empathy—Fiction. 2. Neighbors—Fiction. 3. Schools—Fiction.] I. Title.
PZ7.H231323Jus 2007
[Fic]—dc22
2006017062

ISBN: 978-0-544-64447-2

Manufactured in the United States of America
DOC 10 9 8 7 6 5 4 3 2 1
4500523682

For My Mother,
who is full of grace.

I Did Not Get To Be

1 I did not get to be the helper to Mister Magic the Magician at my very own (so it should have been me) sixth birthday party because Sammy Stringer spit purple grape juice all over my special white shirt with a big six on it, and I had to change it right when Mister Magic was starting up.

Mom said she was sure it was an accident, but I just know that spitting is pretty much an on-purpose thing, and it is almost impossible to forgive someone for something on purpose even if it was almost three years ago, which is a very long time.

Before

After

It Doesn't even look like A "6" Anymore.

2 I did not get to be a singing and dancing corncob in the Thanksgiving play because I was the only girl tall enough to fit into the tree costume who didn't cry real boo-hoo baby tears when she was asked, "Could you please not be a corncob, because what we really, really need is a tree and we already have way more than enough corn-cobs."

I will not say who cried big tears, and is probably a good actress because two seconds after she found out I was going to be the tree she was all smiles, because I am not a tattletale-type person. But I will say that I do not like her even one tiny bit, and that when she is not doing her acting, her true self is a Big Meanie!

Mom said I was a great tree even though I didn't get to say any- thing and Mr. Franks kept whispering at me

I Can See Out But No One Can See Me.

Not A Real Bird

Heavy Arms

Me Inside Tree Costume Standing Perfectly Boringly STILL

to stop moving my arm branches around so much—he didn't think it should be a

Fun Streamer With Real Pieces of Corn on The end.

The Singing And Dancing CornCob looks Beautiful!

windy day. But if you are a tree it is boring to stand there super still with your arms out on each side doing nothing.

3 I did not get to be in the talent night at school and show off the photos I took with my new camera because I was sick with the stomach flu and was throwing up.

my special Red Bucket.. I only use it to Throw Up in. when I am sick.

Aurora Gambit won a first-prize blue ribbon for her photos of flowers, which were okay, but my cat photos are way better

ONE OF MY GREAT CAT PHOTOS

and would have for sure taken her first-prize ribbon right away. Plus, she could be happy with the second-prize ribbon because it is red and that is one of her favorite colors because she says that red things look good with her orangish hair.

Sammy Stringer got an honorable mention green ribbon for his paintings of dog poop, which is totally unbelievable and gross!

4 But the **biggest** I-did-not-get-to-be of my life, ever, happened right at school in front of everybody in the whole third grade class. I did not get to be called Grace, which is an okay thing if your name is Tania or Ruth or Jordan but totally 100 percent unfair if you are me and your name is Grace, which mine is.

I didn't tell Mom because I knew she'd be mad and call the school, and you can't have your mom call the school unless something really bad happens, like maybe someone mean pushes you down and it breaks three of your front teeth, or else everybody will think you are a big baby and a complainer. And I am not either of those two things!

FOUR GRACES IN A ROW

Grace W.

Grace L.

Me

Grace F.
BIG Meanie!

There are four girls named Grace in my class. Miss Lois, our new teacher, said, "We'll have to do something about that. It's too confusing with all you Graces."

Then she said, "Grace Wallace, you will be Grace W. Grace Francis can be Grace F., and Grace Landowski can be Grace L."

Right then Grace L. stood up and said, "Pretty please, Miss Lois, can I be Gracie instead of Grace L.?"

I knew I was next, so I said, "And I want to be just Grace."

"Perfect," said Miss Lois, and then she went down the list of everyone's new names and wrote them in her special book.

"Let's see, we have Grace W., Grace F., Gracie, and Just Grace."

Then Grace F. stood up and started waving her arm like a crazy person, trying to get Miss Lois's attention. She gave me a mean look and said, "How come she gets to be called Grace and I have to be Grace F.? It's not fair! I want to be the one called Grace!" Miss Lois seemed a little grumpy that we were still talking about the Grace name thing.

MISS LOIS BEING GRUMPY

She Has Big Ears Like A Monkey. She can Probably Hear Really Good.

She made a big sigh and said, "You're right, dear—it's not fair for anyone to be called Grace, so that's why Grace Stewart wants to be called Just Grace."

Both Grace F. and I said "Just Grace?" at the same time.

"That's weird!" said Grace F.

I tried to tell Miss Lois that she'd made a mistake and that I wanted to be called just **Grace,**

not **Just Grace,** but she put her hand up in the air and said, "That's enough, girls. Let's move on to the three Owens." And that's how it happened that I have the stupidest name in the whole class! Or maybe even the whole entire world!

Boy Things

1 Spitting and making burping noises.

2 Not caring that your shirt or pants are sticky with food or mud or worse...mucus.

3 Really liking big and flashy superheroes ...the kind with capes.

4 Drawing comics.

There are some girls who do boy things and don't care who knows it. Ruth, a girl in my class from last year, always makes huge burps after she drinks milk. Everyone says it's gross, but you can tell that some of the boys are really impressed, especially Sammy Stringer—he's always trying to learn stuff to become more disgusting.

Then there are other girls who might do boy things but don't want anyone to know. I'm one of those. I don't spit, make burp sounds, or wear disgusting filthy clothes, but when I feel grumpy or sad, it sometimes makes me feel better if I draw a comic. I don't know why it works that way, but it does, and that seems like a good thing.

The day I got my Just Grace name I needed to feel better really fast, so I drew a new Not So Super adventure as soon as I got home. It would have been better to watch an episode of *Unlikely Heroes,* but I'm not allowed to watch TV before dinner.

Not So Super comics are about super- heroes who only have little powers, but still they use them to help people who need it. I got the idea from my favorite TV show in the whole world, *Unlikely Heroes.* Mimi, my best friend ever, says that *Unlikely Heroes* is the kind of show that makes you want to be a better person just by watching it, which is true, and important.

NOT SO SUPER BUT STILL GOOD

My other boy thing is that I sort of have a teeny tiny superpower. It's not a jump-over-buildings, see-through-people's-clothes, or lift-a-train-over-my-head one, which is good, because when you can do those kinds of things you probably have to live in a secret hideout instead of at home with your mom and dad. And I really like my room, so it would be sad to have to move away, so I'm glad I only have a small superpower.

My power is that I can always tell when someone is unhappy, even if that person is pretending to be happy and is a really good actor.

I'M NOT SAD.

My Friend MiMi

DO YOU WANT A PIECE OF MY CANDY?

THANK YOU. I FEEL BETTER.

Me Knowing She is Sad.

She's Really Good At Pretending To Be Okay.

The bad thing about my power is that I always try to do something to make the sad person feel better—even if I should probably leave it alone and not do anything at all. Dad says that feeling people's sadness is called empathy and it's a superpower because of the "having to do something to help them feel better" part. A superhero **has** to help people in trouble. She can't just change into a regular I'm-not-going-to-do-anything-to-help-someone-else type of person even if she wanted to.

**THIS WOULD NEVER HAPPEN
WITH A REAL SUPERHERO**

Rooms You Can Jump In, In My House

1 The bathroom with the broken toilet. Very yucky room.

2 The laundry room. Sometimes when

Mom thinks I have too much energy she tells me to go and jump in the laundry room. I tell her it's no fun to jump in there, plus it's too small. She says, "Why do you have to swing your arms when you jump? There's plenty of room if you jump like a pencil." Then we both laugh because who ever saw a jumping pencil, and she is just being ridiculous.

The reason you can only jump in these two places is that every other room is right above Augustine Dupre's head. Augustine Dupre is the super-amazing French lady who lives in our basement—only the part she lives in doesn't look like a basement, it's a fabulously fantastic apartment.

Dad said she could paint her apartment any way she liked, so she did. Augustine Dupre is not afraid of color. She has a yellow kitchen, an orange bathroom, and a rose-colored bedroom with bright red velvety curtains. It is most truly the coolest place someone could ever live. Dad even bought her apartment a dishwasher, so she doesn't have to wash or dry her dishes by hand like we do.

Augustine Dupre is two times lucky: not only does she have the best apartment ever, but she also has the best job. She is a flight attendant for rich people who travel on airplanes in first class. She could probably go anywhere, but she says her favorite place in the entire whole world is France. Sometimes she even goes there two times in one week.

Mom says not to bother Augustine Dupre with every little thing that's happening in my life, but it's hard not to tell her stuff, because she's a really good listener.

The day I got my Just Grace name I wanted to run downstairs and tell Augustine Dupre all about it right away, but Mom wouldn't let me. Mom said Augustine Dupre was probably tired from flying home from France.

MOM'S SILLY IDEA

OH MY POOR ARMS! THEY ARE SO TIRED. I JUST FLEW IN FROM FRANCE

After dinner I snuck downstairs when Mom wasn't watching. I did my special knock so Augustine Dupre would know it was me. After I told her all about my stupid new name, she said something in French that sounded like she was feeling the empathy thing for me. Then she said that if I wanted she could tell me a very sad story, and that sometimes hearing a very sad story makes your own sad story seem less sad.

I said I wanted to hear it, because I was desperate to feel better about being Just Grace. Sometimes, not knowing what you are asking for can be a mistake. This might have been one of those times.

The Sad Story

Augustine Dupre's story was all about Mrs. Luther, which was a huge surprise. Mrs. Luther is my next-door neighbor and a teacher from my school. A scary old-kid teacher. Dad says that if something scares you it's probably because you don't know all the facts, and that if you learned more facts then you would not be so scared anymore. Dad is wrong!

What I Know About Mrs. Luther The Teacher

1 Wears her glasses on the end of her nose.

2 Teaches the older kids anthropology, which has something to do with understanding strange people from other countries that no one has probably ever heard of before.

3 Looks at you like she has x-ray eyeballs and can see right through to your bones.

4 Has a funny crooked smile, like a

crocodile that has just eaten something cute and furry.

Mrs. Luther

CROCODILE With Mrs. Luther's Hairstyle and Glasses

5 Has just started wearing a big bright orange cast on her leg, so now she walks around holding on to an old-people cane. Bright orange is not a normal grown-up person's color.

What I Know About Mrs. Luther The Neighbor

6 Her house is full of scary-looking masks

hanging all over the walls. I know this because I can see into her living room from my bedroom window. She never closes her drapes, which is not good for me. Creepy masks are not something I like to see at night before I go to sleep, so I always close my eyes while I pull down my window shade.

7 As soon as she gets home from school she puts on a long dress—like a witch dress but it has more colors.

That's seven strange things instead of five. So because Mrs. Luther is my neighbor, I know she is stranger and scarier than the kids at school would ever guess, because they don't even know about her witch dress or the scary masks on her wall. The only not unusual thing I know about Mrs. Luther is her cat, Crinkles. Crinkles is a very nice cat.

I told Augustine Dupre that I thought Mrs. Luther was unusual, which is a word grownups use to mean weird and strange so they won't hurt anyone's feelings, and that it would probably take a lot for me to feel sad for her, even with my extra-sensitive empathy feelings. Augustine Dupre said she was not worried.

What Augustine Dupre Told Me

1 That Mrs. Luther fell off a ladder in her house while she was trying to hang up a new scary mask and almost squashed Crinkles. This is how she broke her leg and why she has to wear a cast. But this does

not explain why it is bright orange instead of a normal grown-up color like white or black.

2 That her son who she loves lives in another country and doesn't call her very much. This is no surprise, because boys do not like to talk on the phone as much as girls.

3 That Mrs. Luther was going to run in a big race and now she can't because she has a broken leg. It is hard to imagine Mrs. Luther wearing a jogging suit, but I don't think she could probably run very fast in her colored witch dress.

4 That her cat, Crinkles, her best friend in the whole world, is now scared of her because he was almost squished by her big

bottom when she fell off the ladder, plus he doesn't like the new orange cast. Augustine Dupre said Mrs. Luther is so sad about this that she cries real tears almost every single night.

The first three things didn't make me feel sad even though missing the big race sounded a lot like my missing my talent night, which was sad for me but I'm not old so it's still okay for me to cry when things like that happen. Old people know how to keep their crying feelings inside. They only let them out when something really bad has happened and they are 100 percent sad. This is why just thinking of Mrs. Luther crying in her house with all those scary masks looking down at her made me feel a little bit sad.

And when Crinkles suddenly jumped on Augustine Dupre's windowsill I got even sadder, because Crinkles is such a lovable cat, and if you had the love of such a great cat it would for sure make you feel the sadness-of-everything-in-the-whole-world not to have it anymore.

Crinkles meowed and meowed until Augustine Dupre went to the window and opened it. She put her finger up to her mouth and made a "shhhh" sound. Crinkles wasn't at all shy. He walked in and jumped right up onto her lap. Augustine Dupre pointed her shushing finger at the ceiling, and I knew exactly what she meant.

One of Dad's big rules is No Pets In The Apartment. He wouldn't even let Augustine

Dupre put a bird feeder outside her window. He said it attracted all the messy neighborhood beasts. He would not be happy to know that Crinkles was a visitor. Sometimes people can be rule breakers if the rules are not good ones and the person who made the rules is not an official-type rule maker who wears a uniform—Dad is not one of those.

Augustine Dupre sighed one of her French sighs (my French teacher at school does this too, so I know it is a French thing) and said, "I don't know how we can make poor Mrs. Luther not so sad. In six weeks when her orange cast comes off, I am sure Crinkles will not be scared of her anymore. Then they will love each other again."

"Is she going to cry every night for six weeks?" I couldn't believe that her sadness could be so big.

Augustine Dupre patted my arm and shook her head, which is a grown-up way of saying, "Yes, I'm sorry to say it, but I believe this to be true."

Superhero Mode

That night before going to bed I looked out my window. I could see Mrs. Luther sitting in one of her big chairs, with all her scary masks looking down at her. I couldn't tell if she was crying. Augustine Dupre was right. I was feeling much less sad about being Just Grace. And even though I am not French, I made a French sigh and thought, *I wonder how I can help Mrs. Luther?* This is how my superhero empathy thing always gets started . . . and once it is going, there is nothing I can do to stop it.

Breakfast

When I am feeling like a superhero I like to have French toast for breakfast; otherwise I just eat a bagel or cereal. If Mom were a detective she would say, "How come you're always up to something when we have French toast for breakfast?" But she isn't, so she says, "French toast? That's a nice change. We haven't had French toast since that time your dad broke his toe."

FRENCH TOAST AND SYRUP

= The Breakfast of SUPER-HEROES

When I got to school I could totally see what the disgusting Sammy Stringer had had for breakfast. It was all over his yellow shirt.

"What's the matter? Do you want

some?" He pointed to a brown sticky part and made smacking sounds with his lips.

I gave him my best I-wish-you-would-melt-into-a-puddle-of-goo look and walked away. Mimi and I have been practicing different looks, because you never know when you might need one. You always have to be ready!

"Just Grace, Just Grace, you are so . . ." Sammy probably couldn't think of a rhyme because he was quiet for too many seconds and then he said, ". . . green."

Green isn't even something silly or clever or funny—it is nothing. So what if I was wearing a green shirt? How Sammy Stringer can be so annoying all the time is a question I will never be able to answer! Sometimes I look at him and I can't help it, but I feel like I hate him and feel a little bit sorry for him both at the same time. I don't like it when the inside parts of you don't match up with what the brain part of you thinks. If there were a medicine to make this go away I would take it, even if it was cherry flavor, which tastes terri- ble and is not my favorite.

What We Are Studying In School That Is Fun

1 Maps and how to draw them—the made-up kind.

MAP OF MY FRIENDS

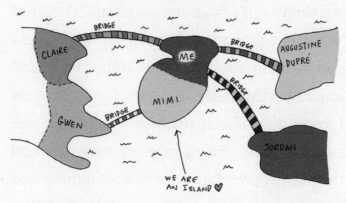

IF THIS WERE A REAL MAP, SAMMY STRINGER WOULD BE SOMEWHERE REALLY FAR AWAY, LIKE OUTER SPACE.

Mimi and I are, of course, best friends, plus we live right next door to each other, so that makes the best friend part even more perfect. Jordan is my best friend in gym class, and she is almost the fastest runner in the whole grade. This is not a good thing if you are "it" and you have to try to catch her. You might think that a real friend would let you catch her sometimes, especially if you are so tired that your eyes might disappear into the back of your head, but Jordan is not that kind of friend. She says, "Try harder." And I do, but then I can't catch her and I say, "Forget it! What is so great about tag anyway?" And then Jordan says, "You're right. I'm tired too." And this is her real friend part, because I know that she is really not tired and she could probably run ten more times around the playground, but I don't say anything and she doesn't say anything and we both sit together and this is good because I am breathing so hard I might almost faint.

Claire is my friend who moved far away, all the way to the ocean. But we can still be friends even though now she lives in California. California is a very beautiful place filled with lots of wonderful things, so I would for sure like to visit her there. She sent me a card and a picture of her standing next to a tree with real oranges on it in her very own backyard. I did not know that oranges grew that way, so there is a lot to learn in California. I am hoping I can visit her sometime soon and miss school. My teachers could not get grumpy and mad about that since I would still be doing lots of learning, only about new California things, which would for sure be much more fun and exciting than regular school learning.

Gwen is Mimi's cousin. I just put her on the map because when she visits Mimi and we are together she is my friend too.

2 Graphs—sort of like percentages if they were in a picture.

3 Percentages—which I already kind of know about from watching *Unlikely Heroes*. They always say things like, "The chance this could happen again is .006 percent," which is like saying almost probably never in a hundred years.

What We Are Studying In School That Is Not Fun

1 The names of all fifty states and where

they are on the map, which is too many to remember even when they are in a song that is supposed to be fun but is not.

2 Spelling, spelling, and more spelling.

3 The life cycle of frogs, which I do not like because they are slimy and one of Sammy Stringer's favorite creatures.

4 The life cycle of a cucumber, which is not exciting for me because I do not like cucumbers or even pickles, which are like tiny cucumbers and maybe even the babies of big cucumbers, but they are still not nice or tasty to eat.

CUCUMBER

I AM FILLED WITH HORRIBLE SEEDS!

FIVE BABIES, WHICH ARE CALLED PICKLES.

I told Mimi all about Mrs. Luther and Crinkles. She is my only friend who knows about the empathy superhero thing. She knows about it so much that she said, "What are you going to do about it?" right when I finished telling her the story.

Sometimes she likes to help out with projects. She says she is happy to just be the helper because if something goes wrong she probably won't get in as much trouble as the leader, which is me.

I didn't have a big plan to tell her about, so I said, "What do you think we should do?"

Sometimes Mimi has good ideas too. She said, "I think we should go to my house and watch *Unlikely Heroes* so we can get some inspirations." *Unlikely Heroes* is her favorite show too. I knew she'd think of something. Plus, Mimi's mom and dad don't have a rule that says no TV before dinner. Super super great!

Supergirl

After school we went to Mimi's house, which is almost like me walking home but then just going next door instead. We practiced some looks, like the I-can't-believe-you-said-that look and the I-think-you-are-disgusting look on each other for a while, and then we watched *Unlikely Heroes*.

This is the most amazing show you could ever watch. Every week they show real live normal people who do superhero things. Once there was a man who lifted a whole car off a lady who was trapped underneath, and then there was a baby who didn't even know how to talk yet but dialed 911 emergency when his mom fainted on the floor. These people are just regular everyday people who suddenly get superpower brains or energy. The bad part for them is that instead of getting to keep the powers all the time they only have them for a little while, like maybe five seconds or ten minutes, and then they are back to being just regular normal no-power people.

The unbelievable best thing is that all the stories are 100 percent really true. Mom says it's a feel-good show, which means that you feel better just watching it. Dad says feel-good shows aren't very popular and that one day soon it will probably be canceled off the TV. I just can't understand why that would happen, but we tape every episode so if it does we can still watch them forever and ever.

Of course we had to watch our favorite episode, where a girl makes a rope out of her clothes and helps pull a grown-up man out of a river before he sinks to the bottom and drowns. She is a hero and only wearing her underwear. The extra-amazing thing is that she just by accident wore her Supergirl undershirt and underpants that day. That makes her being a hero even more I-can-hardly-believe-it!

SUPER GIRL UNDERWEAR

SHE DIDN'T HAVE TO TAKE HER SOCKS OR SHOES OFF.

When it was time for me to go home for supper we still didn't have any good ideas. Mimi even put on her Supergirl T-shirt for inspiration—which is a big word for something that helps make you think of the exact right thing you were hoping to think of—but it wasn't working. I don't have any Supergirl clothes. Not even Supergirl underwear, and I really, really, really want some of those. I could wear them for inspiration thinking and no one would even know. Mom says she is keeping her eye out for them, but that Supergirl underwear isn't that easy to find. I think she is just not trying very hard!

Ways To Not Get A Good Idea

1 Ask your mom or dad.

2 Look in a book that has ideas about how to get ideas.

3 Sit down and think super hard about getting a good idea.

I had tried all of those things at other times and none of them had worked even one tiny bit . . . especially number three. Sometimes it is better to try to just do normal things instead of thinking really hard about getting an idea. Then after a while, the start of a good idea might just pop into your head right at the moment you aren't even thinking about it. It is not good to be thinking, *Is the good idea going to happen in the next two minutes?* That doesn't work either.

Start Of My Big Idea

We had supper and then when we were clearing the table Mom said, "Oh, I forgot to tell you. You got a postcard today. It's on the desk in the hall." How Mom could forget something exciting like a postcard but remember boring things like how many bites of green beans I eat and if I remember to put the toilet lid down is something I hope I'm never going to understand. This is one of the reasons I am not so excited about turning into a grownup. The grown-up world is very filled up with boring rules about eating and cleaning.

The card was from Auntie Bethany. She always sends a postcard when she goes somewhere fun. I like that she is thinking of me when she is having a big adventure. Postcards are the best!!!! It makes my insides feel good to get one. Mom says postcards are old-fashioned. Some old things can be a good idea. Postcards are one of those things. Right when I was reading the part about Auntie Bethany riding a donkey down the Grand Canyon I got the beginning of a good idea. I should send Mrs. Luther postcards, and they should be from . . .

This is What Happens When you Get A Big Idea.

This was the part of the idea that wasn't finished. Who could send the card? I don't know anybody that Mrs. Luther would want to get a card from. It wouldn't be so fun to get a card from me . . . I just live right next door and that is not exciting at all. Who does Mrs. Luther love? Who does she love that I even know? The only answer is Crinkles, but Crinkles is not a person, he is a cat. Cats do not go on exciting holidays, and cats do not write postcards. They can't write anything, even if you helped them and taped a marker to their paw, which would not be such a nice thing to do to a cat that you liked.

Then right when I was thinking about

the marker and the tape I got the rest of the idea. It was perfect. Perfect for me and perfect for Mrs. Luther. It was like a great big Band-Aid. It would fix everything until Mrs. Luther got her cast off.

MR. BAND-AID

My Big Idea

I will send Mrs. Luther postcards from Crinkles, only I will write them and pretend that they are from Crinkles. I will not tape a marker to his paw! Mrs. Luther will be so happy to think that Crinkles is thinking of her even if she really knows for real that it is only pretend, it will make her smile her crocodile smile.

How To Do The Big Idea

1 Take a professional-looking photo of Crinkles and get it blown up big to real cat size. Glue the big photo onto a piece of cardboard. Augustine Dupre can help with this part because she is really good at projects and she will probably be able to make Crinkles sit still so I can take his picture and not have it be all blurry.

2 Take cardboard Crinkles around to different places in town and take his photo there. If I do a good job it will look like the real Crinkles was there instead of the cardboard pretend Crinkles. This will be super cool and funny, because the real Crinkles would never pose in a shopping cart at the grocery store, which is already one of my good ideas about where to take a photo.

3 Glue the photo of cardboard Crinkles onto another piece of cardboard to make a real from-the-store-looking postcard. There is a lot of glue and cardboard in this project, and that makes me worried because it is always hard to get glue to stick in the exact right place you want it to and not have it go all over your fingers or in your hair instead.

4 Mail the postcard, which will not be so hard to do, because Mom has lots of stamps.

I couldn't wait to tell Augustine Dupre all about it. I couldn't wait to hear Mimi say, "Great idea!" I couldn't wait to get started. Too bad it was bedtime.

Superhero Morning

It definitely had to be another French toast breakfast. It takes more than 976 and probably less than 2,000 steps to get to school. I try to count them every morning but always get my attention taken away by something else before I finish. This morning I caught up to Mimi at step number 356, which was okay because it is much more important and fun to talk to her than count steps. She loved my idea and said she couldn't wait to be my helper. She said she is glad I am going to use a cardboard cat because she is very allergic to real cats, which is something I had 100 percent forgotten.

We saw Sammy Stringer and it was too bad but he saw us also. He was riding his bike and delivering newspapers instead of going to school, which is not surprising because our newspaper is always late and Dad usually has to take it on the train with him instead of reading it at breakfast like he likes to do. "Hey, Just Grace, I just delivered your paper." We pretended we didn't hear him. It wasn't fair to call me Just Grace when there weren't even any other Graces around. It was him just being mean and unfair!

Sometimes if Sammy delivers the paper before I leave for school Dad will make me go out to the driveway and get it. I always put on one of Mom's yellow dishwashing gloves first because Sammy is a nose picker and that is disgusting, and you can never tell—he might have done that thing right before he touched our paper.

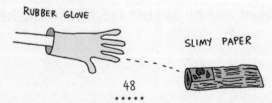

RUBBER GLOVE

SLIMY PAPER

What Happened At School That Was Interesting

1 Mimi had five little tiny sandwiches for lunch instead of one normal-size sandwich. Sometimes little things that are exactly the same as big things are more special and cute (except pickles).

5 MINI SANDWICHES

1 BIG SANDWICH

2 Mrs. Luther had a Band-Aid on her nose, which is something that your eyes have to notice right away. Mimi said she heard that a paperboy had thrown a newspaper at Mrs. Luther's house and that it had hit her in the nose by mistake. And even though it was supposed to be an accident there was no big surprise for me about who the paperboy was. It was Sammy Stringer. Mom said she thought she once saw him try to hit a squirrel with our paper . . . but squirrels are fast. Poor slow Mrs. Luther didn't stand a chance, especially with her broken leg.

SQUIRREL WITH RUNNING SHOES ON

I ran almost all the way home from school. I usually don't have time to count the steps on the way back. I was disappointed that Augustine Dupre wasn't home, but I saw Crinkles sitting under her window. He let me pet him. Too bad I didn't have my camera right then, because he looked extra nice with the sun shining on his fur. Good photographers like to take pictures with real sunlight and not use the flash part of the camera, which is mostly used for inside photos anyway.

HOW TO TAKE A PROFESSIONAL PHOTO

DON'T TAKE A PHOTO OF THE SUN.

SUN IS BEHIND THE PHOTOGRAPHER'S HEAD. THIS IS GOOD.

This is something I learned in the photography book I am reading. It is a very hard book with lots of big words so I usually only read the parts under the pictures. Dad said he is very impressed that I am reading a book from his grown-up book collection.

What Happened At Home That Was Completely Surprising

I was looking out my kitchen window while I was waiting for Augustine Dupre to get home and I saw Sammy Stringer walk up to Mrs. Luther's door. He pushed the door buzzer and then got invited into her house! I ran up to my room and looked out my window, but I couldn't see them in her living room. What he was doing in her house was not something I could even imagine. It was bizarre, which is what they say on *Unlikely Heroes* when something is too hard and not really possible to even understand. I didn't want to think about it, because this kind of thinking usually makes my head hurt, so I drew a new Not So Super comic to try to get my wondering energy away from it.

NOT SO SUPER [BUT STILL GOOD]

I was so busy drawing, I forgot to notice when Augustine Dupre came home. And then it was dinnertime and too late to sneak down to see her.

Mom says she doesn't understand French people, and this is true, because she does not get Augustine Dupre. She understands the words she says but she doesn't know why she says them. Mom says it's a cultural thing, which means that if someone is from another part of the world and you are from here then they might say things that you don't expect, and then you will be confused. I think Mom is wrong, because I can totally understand Augustine Dupre and I have never been to France.

Like the time I gave Augustine Dupre a fake present. I wrapped a lollipop in ten boxes and

← Fancy Bow

Lollipop in 10 Boxes

when she finally got to the end, the last wrapper said "Sucker!"

When Mom found out she got mad and said that it wasn't nice to fool someone that way. She made me go downstairs and apologize, and even though I didn't want to I kind of cried. Augustine Dupre said it was all right and I knew she was telling the truth because she once said, "I'll give you ten dollars if you can whistle in the next two minutes while eating these five crackers." I tried and tried but there is no way you can whistle with a mouth full of salty crackers, so she knows how to play a joke too!

THIS IS SOMETHING YOU CANNOT DO

It is much easier to go downstairs and visit when Mom is busy making supper. After dinner she has more time to be watching what I am doing. But tonight I was lucky. Her favorite crime show was on and it was one of those loud noisy ones with lots of sirens, crying, and shooting. She didn't pay any attention to me when I snuck downstairs.

I told Augustine Dupre all about Sammy Stringer, all about Mrs. Luther, and all about my big idea. She said she was in love with my idea and that she would of course be happy to help me. The whole time we talked about it she was petting Crinkles. That cat has given all his Mrs. Luther love to Augustine Dupre. You can just tell it by the way he looks at her when she scratches him behind his ears. He is filled with love for her . . . poor

Mrs. Luther is definitely triple-wounded.

Today it was raining, which was bad and good. Bad because I couldn't take a professional-looking photo of Crinkles outside with the sun shining down on his fur, but good because I am happy to know that Sammy Stringer will have to ride his bike in the rain and get soaking wet while he is delivering papers. This is not just me being mean—he deserves to be wet and unhappy! Plus, the rain will wash away any disgusting germs he leaves on the plastic newspaper bag before anyone else has to touch it! But I will still wear my rubber glove, just to be safe.

What I Almost Could Not Believe

At school today Sammy Stringer was telling everybody that he had a friend who had a collection of bugs bigger than his hand and a jar filled with real live African lion poop.

A NORMAL-SIZE HAND BUT NOT
A NORMAL-SIZE BUG

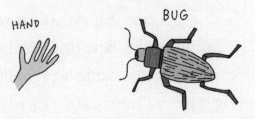

HAND

BUG

Of course no one was believing him. No one except me. Though I didn't think he was being completely full of truthfulness by calling Mrs. Luther his friend. For sure they didn't share sips from the same cup, give each other cheer-up hugs, or swear to keep real important things secret, which are all things that are done by a real 100 percent for real friend.

But I didn't say anything because I didn't want anyone and mostly him to think that I was taking his side. Sammy Stringer and I are not and will never be friends! Mimi said she was glad her dad bought his paper at the train station so they didn't have to have a paperboy. I told her I wished I could say that too.

Liar, Liar I Wish Your Pants Were On Fire

Grace F. was her usual Big Meanie self today and was trying to make up as many reasons as she could to call me Just Grace in front of every person in the entire class. When Miss Lois asked her about the capital city of Wisconsin she said, "Oh, I can't remember, but I think Just Grace has a cousin that lives there." This was totally untrue and just a big lie, because I don't have any cousins, and even if I did I would never tell Grace F. one single thing about them, especially where they lived.

So before she could say another made-up thing about me I said, "She's lying! I do not have any cousins in that state or even in the entire world."

Miss Lois gave me one of her concentration looks and said, "Just Grace, you know better than to speak out without raising your hand. Do you know what city is the capital of Wisconsin?" Of course I could not think of the right answer to that question, plus,

Wisconsin is such a hard name to remember all by itself. When I thought about it, it filled up my brain and there was not even enough room left for a probably impossible-to-remember city name as well. Miss Lois was still staring at me and I couldn't think of anything to say that she would like to hear. Miss Lois looked back and forth at me and the Big Meanie, and then she said, "Well, girls, as homework you two can do some research on Wisconsin, and when you come back on Monday you can tell the class two interesting facts about the state as well as the name of the capital city."

"Are we doing it together?" The Big Meanie gave me a if-I-have-to-work-with-you-I-will-throw-up look.

"Sure, if you girls want to work together you can," said Miss Lois. This time I put my hand up. "I don't want to, *thank you*," I said, and I mean-looked right back at Grace F.! Instead of "thank you" what I wanted to say was "even if I were almost the last person in the whole world and all my friends were dead and Grace F. were the only person I would get to talk with for a whole month, or even a year, I still would 100 percent not want to work with her!" But you can't say stuff like that in a class in front of a teacher and not get in trouble.

Miss Lois shook her head like she does when she seems confused and does not understand what is going on. She probably thinks that all the Graces should be friends. She does not get that some Graces are nicer and better than other Graces.

When I looked behind me I could see that Sammy Stringer was looking right at me and smiling, with something gross stuck on his front tooth. I hoped that it was on purpose, because I don't know why, but something stuck on your tooth by accident seems a lot grosser.

The Completely Surprising Thing Happens Again

After school I saw Sammy Stringer get invited into Mrs. Luther's house again. I am not spying on Mrs. Luther and definitely not spying on Sammy Stringer, but every time I look out the window I just see them. I can understand why Sammy Stringer would think that Mrs. Luther is cool—she has that lion poop collection, which is probably making him crazy with excited joy. He just loves poop.

But the reason Mrs. Luther would like him is harder to figure out. She could just be super, super, super, super lonely or else she could be doing one of those anthropology studies on Sammy. The kind where she studies strange people that live in countries that no one has ever heard of before. Only Sammy lives here, but he is so strange so maybe that part doesn't matter.

And Then...

I tried to draw a Not So adventure so that I wouldn't use all my concen-

MRS. LUTHER STUDYING SAMMY. SHE IS WRITING THINGS DOWN.

tration on Mrs. Luther and Sammy Stringer, but I couldn't do it.

Sometimes it's not very easy to stop yourself from thinking of something once your brain has started thinking about that thing. I drew Sammy Stringer and Mrs. Luther even though they were the exact things I was trying not to think about.

If You Hear Some Strange Noises Out Your Window You Should Probably Look And See What It Is

Mrs. Luther was standing on her porch, shouting at Sammy. At first I thought she was mad at him, which wasn't so hard to imagine to be true, but then I could tell that she was yelling directions. "Run to the left. Now go straight. No, wait, quick—run to the right."

Sammy was wearing two big red oven mitts over his hands and was flapping his arms up and down, over and over again. He was running like crazy all over Mrs. Luther's yard, just like one of those giant ostriches they have at the zoo. At the zoo you have to be careful and not get too close or they'll peck you in the eye. Ostriches like shiny things like coins and eyeballs. Mrs. Luther might have put a spell on him and changed his brain to think he was an ostrich. Sometimes if something is bad for the person who it is happening to it can still be funny if you are the one watching and it is not you running around like a big crazy bird.

OSTRICH   **BOY**

But it was maybe not so funny if Sammy Stringer was going to think he was an ostrich forever. That would be bad, even for someone I did not like. Then when I saw Crinkles run under a bush, I knew what was the truth. Sammy Stringer was trying to catch Crinkles. Why he was doing it with big red oven mitts must have been a secret cat-catching reason. If Crinkles didn't like Mrs. Luther's orange cast, it didn't seem that he would be happy to be grabbed by big flapping red oven mitties.

"Go left! He's right there on your left!" shouted Mrs. Luther. She was waving her arms and jumping up and down at the top of her steps, which is maybe something you should not do with a big orange cast on your leg. Crinkles ran right past Sammy, through the fence and into our yard. I could tell he was going to exactly the place where he was not supposed to go. I was right about the cast and jumping, because the next time I looked at the steps Mrs. Luther was lying on them and Sammy was trying to help her up. She stood up and shooed Sammy's help away.

All the fun was over. Crinkles was gone, Mrs. Luther was limping like normal, and Sammy was not being Ostrich Boy. I ran downstairs and found Crinkles just where I knew he would be. I would make a good cat detective. Crinkles was sitting on Augustine Dupre's table, drinking milk from one of her very fancy French teacups—the ones that always make me feel special and nervous to touch because they look like they could break into a million pieces really easy.

"Crinkles is very upset. He jumped in the window and wouldn't stop meowing, so I gave him some milk to calm him down. I think his fear of Mrs. Luther is getting worse," said Augustine Dupre. "I am getting very worried." She petted Crinkles behind his ears. Crinkles did not look upset at all. He looked very happy.

I told her all about Sammy, Mrs. Luther, and the big red oven mitts. "This is very strange, very strange indeed," said Augustine Dupre, and she picked up Crinkles and held him close. She didn't say anything else, but it seemed like maybe Augustine Dupre was in love with Crinkles too!

The Bad Thing Augustine Dupre Told Me

Augustine Dupre told me she had to leave the next day on an emergency trip to France, and that it could not be helped, but the sad truth was she would be gone for two whole weeks. She would not be around to help with any part of my big idea! Not the taking-the-photo-of-Crinkles part, not the blowing-up-the-picture part, and not the gluing part. Nothing!

I tried to talk to her about what to do next, but she was not being a good listener like she normally is. She was putting all her clothes into little piles and doing lots of French sighing that had nothing to do with me or Crinkles. Crinkles went and sat right in the middle of Augustine Dupre's suitcase, like he was hoping that she was going to take him to France with her, but she said she would not do a thing like that even though she would miss him.

I could tell Crinkles was hoping that she was lying to me. He wanted to go anywhere Augustine Dupre was going to go. He was in love.

Taking The Photo Of Crinkles

Today was a beautiful sunny day. It was perfect outside weather to take a picture of Crinkles, and that was too bad because Augustine Dupre, my big helper, was gone. When you are going to France you have to get up and leave really early in the morning.

After breakfast, which was not French toast because Mom said she was tired of it and so we had to have pancakes instead, I went outside to find Crinkles. He was walking around in our front yard. I was happy to see that he was not on his way to France with Augustine Dupre, but I was not happy about how he was not being at all helpful with my project.

No matter how hard I tried and tried, and talked to him in a nice, not mad voice, he was still not a good photo subject. Every time I put him in a perfect sit-up pose, the second I stepped back to take the photo he'd lie down and roll all over the ground the way he does when he wants to be petted. He would not stay sitting up. And then even after I petted him for maybe ten minutes, he still wanted more pets. I cannot believe that he is that lonely and misses Augustine Dupre already. He is a very needy cat. This is the kind of thing you say when you are talking about someone who takes up all your energy and never seems full.

Finally, I just had to wait for him to stand up and then take his picture when he was walking. It was not excellent, but he still looked nice with the sun shining on his fur. He is a very nice-looking cat. In photography language, someone who looks good in photos gets to be called photogenic. Crinkles is photogenic.

THE POSE I WANTED   **THE POSE I GOT**

Mom drove me to the photocopy store.

If she thinks I am doing a project for school she is always happy to help. I didn't say my project was not for school and she didn't ask if my project was for school, so we both were thinking different things were the truth. When this kind of thing happens it is called a miscommunication. It is not a lie, and this is good because I am not a liar.

Mom doesn't like to stand around inside the copy store, so she took a magazine and waited in the car, which was good for me, because she would for sure want to know why I needed a cat-size picture of Crinkles if she saw it. She would not understand my project.

The lady in the store was helpful about blowing up the Crinkles photo. Her name was Chuck, which is usually a boy's name, but that is what her nametag on her apron said. Chuck said that Crinkles looked like a very nice cat and I said he was, but I did not tell her more because I did not want one more lady to fall in love with him. I got two big pictures of Crinkles in case I made a mistake, because the cutting and gluing is always hard to do right.

CARDBOARD CRINKLES

Looking at cardboard Crinkles made me smile. I couldn't wait for Mimi to come over and see him. She would love him like she could never love a real cat, and that would be a great thing for her.

Tomorrow we were going to make a plan about where to take the pictures. Mimi said she would be happy to help make cardboard Crinkles stand up in all sorts of places. It was something I was so excited about that I could hardly go to sleep. Cardboard Crinkles slept in my closet, and I could not believe how real he looked every time I opened the door to check on him. Everything was going to work out just perfect, I could tell.

What I Learned About Wisconsin Before Mimi Came Over

I had to do my Wisconsin homework before Mimi came over. That is what Mom said, and then she said she was going to check it, which means I had to do a good job and not just write down some stuff real hasty, which is her favorite word for meaning not taking time to do something properly.

My first fact was about the National Freshwater Fishing Hall of Fame. A fishing museum does not sound very exciting, except for the special fact that outside the museum is a supersize giant fish that you can climb up into. You can even stand in its mouth and wave at the people down on the ground in the parking lot. It is the world's biggest not real muskie, which is good because if it was a real fish it would probably be the biggest monster fish in the lake.

ME WAVING FROM INSIDE A MUSKIE

HIGH IN
THE AIR

My second fact about Wisconsin was the circus parade, which happens right through the middle of a city called Milwaukee. At the end of the parade the circus people give out rides on the elephants, camels, and zebras. I don't know if this can be true, because I have never seen a person ride a zebra, but I hope that it is real, because a zebra ride sounds very fun and like something I would be happy to have a photo of.

ME WAVING ON THE BACK OF A ZEBRA

Some other facts about Wisconsin are the state insect, which is the honeybee, and the invention of the first ice cream sundae in a city called Two Rivers. These are not as exciting as my first two facts, which I am hoping that Grace F. does not pick. I will be mad if she gets to go first and she chooses the same two interesting facts about Wisconsin as I have, and then tells about them like they are hers.

Mimi Is In Love

Mimi never gets to go near real cats, so she was super excited to hold Crinkles. I took a picture of her with him and in the camera it looked like she was holding a real cat. She said she was in love with cardboard Crinkles, which was okay because it was not the real Crinkles, who already had too much love in his cat life.

After we made a map and a plan, because it is always good to know what you are doing so mistakes will not happen, Mimi and cardboard Crinkles and I went outside to take the photos. We did not see the real Crinkles, for which Mimi was glad.

MAP OF WHERE TO TAKE THE PHOTOS OF CRINKLES

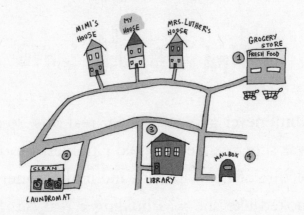

Cardboard Crinkles was a great photo subject—he stood still and never looked away or flopped down when he was supposed to be standing up. When we took the picture of Crinkles in the shopping cart at the grocery store, a man came by and asked about our cat. He thought cardboard Crinkles was real! Mimi was so excited, she couldn't stop jumping up and down.

We couldn't wait to get home and get the pictures out of the camera to make the postcards. Dad has shown me how to do this with the computer, and it is pretty easy if you don't press any of the wrong keys on the keyboard. Usually I am allowed to use the computer only when Dad is there to help, but I knew just what to do already, so it was okay. The computer always asks you lots of questions, and as long as you don't say yes when it asks you about the word *delete*, things will not go really bad. Really bad is when Dad uses lots of grown-up words that I am not allowed to say, and then he has to talk for forever on the phone to a computer person who tries to help him fix what is wrong. This makes Dad very grumpy, mad, and not a fun dad. I did not want this to happen.

POSTCARD NUMBER ONE

Hi! I was thinking of you and how you love going to the grocery store! Maybe I could come with you sometime!

Love,
Crinkles

Mrs. Luther
782 Marshfield Lane
Morgan, N.J.

Writing the postcard was not very easy, and not as fast as we thought it would be. There was a lot of hard stuff to figure out right at the start of the postcard. "Dear Mrs. Luther" sounded too official-like, and we decided that "Human Mommy" sounded too weird—like maybe Crinkles was an alien or something. That's why we had to just write "Hi." It was the only thing that would work.

After that we had to decide why Crinkles would want to send a postcard from the grocery store in the first place. Projects sure get a lot more complicated once you are really doing them and not just thinking about doing them.

Writing postcard number two was easier because most of the hard stuff was already figured out from doing postcard number

**POSTCARD
NUMBER
TWO**

DROP OFF SERVICE
7AM - 8PM   MON. - FRI.
8-5PM   SAT. & SUN.

Hi again! So this is
where you take my
favorite cozy blanket to
be washed. I miss not
being cozy with you.
                Love,
            Crinkles

Mrs. Luther
782 Marshfield Lane
Morgan, N.J.

one. Mimi did the writing on the postcard just in case Mrs. Luther would recognize my handwriting style since I lived right next door to her.

Mimi wanted to write all the postcards at once, but I said this would not be a good idea, because then it would be too hard to not mail them all right away. When something is super fun, it is hard to make yourself stop doing that something, even if you say, "We should not do this super-fun thing anymore." And then what would happen is that Mrs. Luther would get all her postcards on the same day, which was not the way the big idea was supposed to go. Mimi made me promise that we could make some more postcards tomorrow. And she made me promise that I would not put any more in the mailbox if she was not with me.

These were not hard promises to make, because Mimi is my best friend and it is always more fun to do stuff with her than to do stuff by myself. I could hardly keep my joy inside me, I was so excited. We ran to the mailbox and mailed postcard number one. I couldn't wait for Mrs. Luther to get it and start feeling better right away. This is my favorite part of being a sort-of superhero.

Wisconsin And Lion Poop

Grace F. did not get to go first about telling two interesting facts about Wisconsin. This was like a big present for me. Miss Lois said she was very impressed about my Wisconsin discoveries and said that an elephant ride sounded like an exciting thing to try. This was kind of a surprise, since I could not even imagine Miss Lois riding on a bicycle, which is a more normal thing to ride than an elephant.

Grace F. seemed really mad when it was her turn and said that her number one interesting fact about Wisconsin was the giant muskie, but that since I had already used it up she didn't want to talk about it again. I said, "Well, you can tell about the honeybee or the ice cream sundae. I didn't use those ones."

"Just Grace! What have I told you about speaking out of turn without raising your hand!" Miss Lois was mad at me.

"She's ruined it! Now I don't have one single thing to tell about Wisconsin! She told everything!" Grace F. was mad too. She was pointing at me, and she was talking, and she was not raising her hand.

Miss Lois was shaking her head again. "Okay, girls. Let's just all calm down." Then

WASP

MEAN

she made Grace F. tell us her two facts even though I had already told about them. When she said the honeybee was the insect of Wisconsin, she did not say that honeybees and wasps are not the same thing and that it can be con-fusing to tell the difference. This is something I would have said, but I was not going to help her with her part of the project anymore.

HONEYBEE

FRIENDLY

Sammy brought lion poop in a glass jar for his show and tell for animal week. Most people bring books about animals or a photo of their favorite pet. I am certain that no one in the entire class has ever brought real poop to school before. Everybody except me was impressed. What is so great about lion poop? Even Miss Lois seemed impressed, which was the second surprise I had about her in one day.

Sammy looked over and smiled at me. I did not smile back. I did not want him to think that I shared his joy about animal poop, which I certainly do not. Olivia Berchelli brought in a picture of her cat, Pookie. Sammy Stringer put his hand up and said, "I don't like cats." This was a not nice thing to say and also a very strange thing to say, since a lion is really just a very big cat. It is hard for me to think nice things about him. He is too much hard work.

Spying For A Good Reason Is Not Bad

As soon as I got home from school I ran up to my room to look out my window. I was hoping I would see Mrs. Luther smiling and holding up my postcard, but instead I saw nothing. Her drapes were closed! This was very mysterious and confusing. She had never closed the drapes before. What was she doing in there? A dance of joy or a dance of sadness and crying? I couldn't decide what to think.

Augustine Dupre was not around to talk to, and I did not feel like drawing a comic, and I could not watch TV because it was before dinnertime, so I went outside for a walk around the house. Maybe Mrs. Luther was outside too. She was not. Even Crinkles was not.

Walking around the house is not a very interesting thing to do if you do it more than three times in a row. I closed Augustine Dupre's window, which she had left open by mistake, and went back inside.

WALKING AROUND HOUSE

3 TIMES AROUND THE HOUSE

I called Mimi and told her we had to have an emergency mailing and mail postcard number two right away. She couldn't come over, so I had to go do it by myself. It was not as much fun as mailing postcard number one. Then there was nothing more to do. Just wait. Waiting is not fun no matter where you are. It is always mostly boring and long, even if you try to find something to do.

After dinner we all watched a new episode of *Unlikely Heroes*. Mom is right! It is a feel-good show. It made me feel so much better.

Trouble

Sammy Stringer is in trouble. He took the glass jar with the lion poop from Mrs. Luther's house without asking her permission. This is stealing, but Sammy said he was just borrowing it, which is probably true but

still bad if you do it without asking.

The principal made
Sammy go and give it back
to Mrs. Luther, and then
he had to apologize to her.

LION POOP IN JAR

The worst thing about this
is that he had to do it in front of her class,
which was filled up with all the big kids.
Some of them were being mean and laugh-
ing until Mrs. Luther made them all be quiet.
This is probably what made Sammy cry, all
the big kids being quiet and watching him. It
is really hard to say you're sorry when you
are trying to stop your eyes from crying in
front of lots of people you don't know. Poor
Sammy.

After the whole thing happened he had
to go to the nurse's office for a while to calm
himself down and try to make his face not

look like it had been crying. He is going to know that we all know he cried, even if we pretend we don't know a thing about it. It is going to be hard for him to walk around and pretend everything is normal when it most certainly is not. I was feeling sad for him. I couldn't help it. When he came back to our class I turned around, and when he looked at me I smiled. This was probably a bad idea, but I had to do it.

More Postcards

After school Mimi came over and we glued two more postcards together. Writing the message on the back is the most fun part. We signed these ones with a big heart next to the pawprint so that Mrs. Luther would know

POSTCARD NUMBER THREE

There are so many really
good books about cats here.
Did you ever know that one
of my favorite things is
books about cats? One of my
other favorite things is you!

 Love,
Crinkles

Mrs. Luther
782 Marshfield Lane
Morgan, N.J.

POSTCARD NUMBER FOUR

This is how I send my
postcards to you. I hope
you like them.
    I miss you!

        Love,
    Crinkles

Mrs. Luther
782 Marshfield Lane
Morgan, N.J.

that Crinkles loved her. Even though I am a little bit mad at Mrs. Luther for making Sammy cry in front of the big kids, we still mailed postcard number three. She probably didn't know he was going to cry, so maybe it wasn't so much her fault.

Mimi wanted me to take more photos of her with Crinkles, but I had an even better idea—I told her she could have the extra cardboard Crinkles to take home. She was so happy, she hugged and hugged me until I had to tell her to stop, because it was not feeling so nice to be hugged so much. Too many hugs is not a good thing. It is too bad that she has her allergy. I can just tell that she would love real cats if she could get close to them. I am extra lucky that way.

It Was A Bad Idea

Smiling at Sammy Stringer yesterday was a bad idea. Today he was smiling back at me every single time I just-by-accident looked at him. He probably thinks I like him and that we are going to be friends. All because I gave him a teeny tiny I-feel-sorry-for-you smile yesterday. If he thinks we will have lunch together and pick each other as partners in gym class, he is totally wrong. I would never give up Jordan, who is my best gym friend, and even if she went on vacation to Hawaii, like she is going to do in two months, I would still not pick Sammy Stringer as my gym partner. I would for sure pick someone else instead.

Sammy's smile-at-me would not go

away! It smiled at me for the whole entire school day! I could not get rid of it no matter how hard I tried, and even after I mean-looked at him, it was still there. I was glad to go home!

Spying Is Hard

After school I saw Mrs. Luther on her front porch. She was carrying lots and lots of papers, so I couldn't tell if some of them were my postcards. I also couldn't tell if she looked happy. She was having a lot of trouble holding on to all her stuff while she was try-ing to open her front door. It's probably not good to watch someone have trouble and not do anything about it, but I didn't want her to know I was spying on her. I wish she would open her drapes so I could see if she looks happy when she is inside her house.

I went outside and walked to the mailbox on the corner to mail postcard number four. Mimi said it would be okay if I did it by myself. If this one doesn't work I don't know what else we can do.

There was no one outside anywhere. I didn't even see Crinkles. He might be hiding and sad because Augustine Dupre is in France. I am starting to get sad about that too. I thought that Crinkles and I could maybe be sad about that together, but he is not around, so we will both have to be sad alone instead. This project is not working as perfectly as I thought it would. I made some Not So Super comic drawings in my notebook, but it did not cheer me up even one little bit.

SUPERHERO IDEAS

Trouble Times Two

Sammy is in trouble again. He got called into the principal's office right in the middle of reading class, which is a very unusual thing to happen. Jordan was in the nurse's office right next door. She tripped while she was running and hurt her ankle, so she got to miss reading class. It is much more fun to read in the nurse's office because the nurse has lots of magazines to look at and for some reason Miss Lois says, "Magazines are not the same as books and they don't count for reading," so we don't get to have them in our classroom.

BOOK VERSUS MAGAZINE

BOOK VS. MAGAZINE

WORDS AND
MAYBE SOME
PICTURES

PHOTOGRAPHS, WORDS,
AND PICTURES

Jordan told Mimi and me all about Sammy's trouble when she came back from the nurse's office at lunchtime. Jordan said the principal was in the office with Mrs. Luther and she got to hear everything they said to Sammy, but she could not understand what Sammy said back because he was crying and it was too hard to understand him.

What they are thinking is so crazy that I cannot believe they would think such a thing could be true. They think that Sammy catnapped Crinkles to be mean to Mrs. Luther because she got mad at him for stealing the lion poop. Mrs. Luther said that Crinkles has been missing for two days and it is not like him to not come home to eat, even if he is scared of her orange cast. When they said, "Revenge is a serious crime," Sammy started crying so hard, they had to make him breathe into a paper bag so he wouldn't choke and die. After that they called his mom to come to the school and get him.

BREATHE IN AND OUT IN THE PAPER BAG. IT HELPS CALM YOU DOWN.

"I knew that Sammy Stringer was no good!" said Mimi.

"He's disgusting and mean!" said Jordan.

"That's true," I said. "But he doesn't like cats." I remembered in my imagination him flapping around Mrs. Luther's yard with the big red oven mitts over his hands.

"Exactly," said Jordan. "He's a catnapper!"

"Poor Crinkles," said Mimi, and she looked like she was going to cry.

"No! He doesn't like cats because he's scared of them! He's a scaredy-cat. But scared of cats! He wouldn't hurt Crinkles. He's probably even too chicken to touch him." I was just like one of those super-smart detectives on Mom's TV crime show. They always put their hands on their hips when they have finished solving a very

tricky crime, so I did it too. "Ta-da!" I said. "He is innocent!"

"Ta-da," said Jordan, "he is not! They have proof! Sammy sent Mrs. Luther ransom notes that had cat photos on them and everything. He even made her cat sit in a grocery cart. So see? He had to touch it!"

Trouble For Me

It is no fun getting in trouble, and it is very much no fun knowing that you are going to be in trouble, even if the trouble part hasn't happened yet. Mimi and I didn't know what we were going to do. I knew that Mimi didn't catnap Crinkles and she knew that I didn't catnap Crinkles, but we knew that it was us that had sent the ransom notes, only they weren't ransom notes but feel-good postcards. And right now they were not making me or her feel very good.

I wasn't feeling so bad for Sammy Stringer anymore—I was feeling more bad for me! He was going to be fine. He probably hadn't done any more wrong things at all.

I wished some kind of empathy superhero could come along to save me. I wanted it really bad, but even if you close your eyes and wish real hard for superhero help, nothing is going to happen, so I kept my eyes open.

And then, because we had to, because we are good people, Mimi and I went to the principal's office by ourselves, on purpose, and told Mr. Harris, our principal, everything.

After we finished our explaining of the big idea, Mr. Harris was not as mad as we thought he was going to be. I was feeling good that I did not cry and that Mimi did not cry. Crying is something that sometimes happens even if you don't want it to. It is hard to keep control of it and make it not happen.

Mr. Harris said he was glad that we had been filled up with lots of "good intentions." These are the I'm-sure-this-is-the-perfect-thing-to-do feelings you have right before you do something to help someone else. Real superheroes must have a lot of these.

Mrs. Luther was not as glad about the "good intentions" as Mr. Harris was. She looked at us like we were maybe not 100 percent telling her the truth. She said it was troubling and strange how Crinkles disappeared right when we started sending her the postcards.

We nodded our heads to say, "Yes, you are right, that is very strange and very troubling," but that didn't make her any happier. The way Mrs. Luther was being made me think that maybe she was not the kind of person who deserved the feel-good postcards in the first place. She was making me have bad feelings about my empathy superhero powers, which is not a good thing to feel.

Then Mrs. Luther surprised us and said, "I'm relieved none of this had anything to do with Sammy Stringer. He really is quite an interesting boy, very curious. I must apologize to him."

BEFORE APOLOGY   AFTER APOLOGY

Grownups hardly ever say they are sorry to kids, and I don't think I have ever heard of a teacher doing an apology to a student before. Mrs. Luther gave us one more look and then walked away to go say she was sorry to Sammy Stringer. He was going to be shocked and surprised!

Mimi was right. The helper does not get in as much trouble as the number one planner.

Mr. Harris said he had to call my dad to explain everything, not because he wanted to get me in trouble but just because parents had a right to know certain things and this was one of those certain things. And I knew that it was exactly the kind of certain thing that Dad and Mom would not understand and do lots of loud talking about, which would end up with me getting in trouble.

Mr. Harris didn't call Mimi's dad. He said that dad could drop Mimi off at her house on our way home.

Thing I DiD Not Get In Trouble For

Wanting to help someone else. Dad said this is an important thing, but not so important that it makes all the other things I did get in trouble for disappear right out of his memory. This is too bad, because if that happened I would not be getting in trouble and would maybe be getting a medal or something instead.

Things I Got In Trouble For

1 Making Mom take me to the copy store for a project that was not for school.

This was not really fair, since it is impossible to make Mom do anything she does not want to do, but when I said this Mom said, "Do not press your luck, young lady!" and then I didn't say anything more because when Mom calls me "young lady" she is really mad. This I know from when it has happened before.

NAMES MOM CALLS ME WHEN SHE IS ANGRY

YOUNG LADY!
GRACE STEWART!
MISSY!

2 Using the computer and the expensive photo paper without asking Dad.

Dad did not act really really mad about this, and I could tell that he was maybe a little bit proud that I had done so much computer work all by myself without anything going wrong. Mom was standing right next to him so he had to pretend to be mad, and she did not see him wink at me.

3 Walking all over the neighborhood without telling Mom and Dad where I was going.

This was the biggest get-in-trouble of all, and when they were saying it I wished I were invisible and could sneak away so I wouldn't have to hear how worried sick they said they would have been if they had known what I was doing, even though it was over and I was standing right in front of them, 100 percent perfectly fine. Making your parents worried sick is not a good feeling.

4 Dad said all the other things in one sentence, so that means that they were small troubles and nothing he was going to remember forever and ever until I was all grown up, like the other stuff. These things were taking the stamps without asking, spying on Mrs. Luther, and being a bad example to Mimi. I know that Mimi does not need me to help her be a bad example, but I did not say that right then because it was not a good way to get the trouble-talk to stop.

STAMPS TALKING

The almost worst part about the whole getting-in-trouble was that Dad said I had to walk over to Mrs. Luther's house and apologize for the postcards all over again, even though I already said I was sorry to her at school. Dad even came with me to make sure I did it right.

I was hoping and hoping that Mrs. Luther would not be home, but I was not lucky about that, because she answered the door in her rainbow witch dress. I said, "I'm really sorry about the postcards." And then Mrs. Luther said, "That's all right, dear. I suppose it's

MRS. LUTHER'S WITCH DRESS

quite flattering that you went to so much trouble, isn't it?" Which was something I did not understand but I nodded "yes" because yes is mostly the right answer if you are confused by a grownup's question and the grownup is smiling when she asks you. If she is not smiling, then the answer is probably no.

Then Mrs. Luther asked Dad if he had seen the postcards, and when he said no she went to get them. I asked Dad if I could go home, because I was standing there 100 percent sure that seeing the postcards was going to make him all mad again. He said, "You are not to move," which means, "No, you cannot go home," but it does not mean I have to be perfectly like a statue still.

Dad Is Not So Mad

Dad and Mrs. Luther talked, and talked, and talked about the postcards and how wonderful they looked. Dad said he could not believe that it was not Crinkles standing in the shopping cart. I was trying not to smile, so I looked at the ground and Mrs. Luther's scary masks behind her. Not smiling is hard to do, but when you are in trouble it is better to stay looking sad so you won't have to get told again about how much trouble you are in. When you are in trouble, looking sad and unhappy for a pretty long time makes your parents think you are very, very, sorry.

On the way home Dad said, "I'm very impressed with you, but that does not mean you are not in trouble and grounded for one week."

Revenge

Mrs. Luther is not friendly! Yesterday she was only pretending to be nice, because last night I am 100 percent sure that she sent some ghosts over to my house to punish me. I heard them when it was dark and I was sleeping. They were making scary spooky sounds right near my room!

SLEEPING CHAIR

Mom and Dad let me sleep in their room on the big chair in the corner. I think Mom whispered to Dad that she heard something too, but she didn't make him put on his clothes to go outside and look around.

In the morning Dad looked in my room

and outside my window but he couldn't find anything creepy or scary. The only thing he found was Sammy Stringer, who was poking around in our yard. Dad invited Sammy to come inside our house, which I could not believe! And it was right when I was eating breakfast, so Dad asked him if he wanted some pancakes too. I had to sit across from the disgusting Sammy Stringer and watch him eat food, at my very own breakfast table!

Dad said, "Your friend Sammy here was outside looking for Mrs. Luther's cat. Maybe after breakfast you'd like to give him a hand? You seem to know all about that cat. It'd be nice to get that poor woman back her pet."

Mom came downstairs and gave Sammy and me one of her super-big surprised looks. I was mad at Sammy Stringer for getting invited into my very own house and eating my very own pancakes right in front of me, so I said, "How come you're not wearing your red oven mitts?"

HOW SAMMY SHOULD EAT PANCAKES

SAMMY EATING PANCAKES
WITH OVEN MITTS.
HA! HA!

I was not going to be nice, even if I did save him from trouble because I couldn't help but do it, and even if he was in my house.

"I'm not going to touch the cat, I'm just going to find him. Mrs. Luther said if I could find him she would let me have that jar of lion poop for my collection and I could keep it forever."

"Well, that's certainly a prize!" said Mom. I don't know how she could smile so nice and not make a disgusted face like I did —she is really good at pretend faces.

"I'll tell you what," said Dad, pointing at me. "You two do a team-up and find that cat and I'll forget about the grounding. Deal?"

"Deal!" said Sammy even though it was not his deal, because Dad was not even talking to him. He was talking to me.

"Great," said Dad. And Sammy Stringer smiled at me with his mouth sort of open, so I could see all the bits of pancakes in between his teeth.

Forced Partner

Sammy wanted to do lots of talking and acting like we were friends on a special cat-finding mission, but I told him right away the truth.

I said, "Sammy Stringer, I am not going to be your friend. I am only doing this cat project with you because my dad says I have to."

"Me too!" said Sammy, but then he wouldn't be quiet and kept asking me all about how I made the postcards, and if I was going to make any more. I don't think he has very good understanding skills!

We looked all over Mrs. Luther's yard and all over my yard, and even in Mimi's yard, which did not make me happy, because I did not want Mimi to see me with Sammy Stringer, even if I was not talking and being friends with him. We looked and looked and looked, but we did not find Crinkles.

I broke my don't-talk-to-Sammy rule and said, "I guess Crinkles ran away. Mrs. Luther is just too scary for him to be around."

"She's not scary," said Sammy, and he was looking at me like he could not understand what I was saying. "She's really cool and interesting, plus, she makes the best cookies ever because they have . . . Hey! What's that sound?"

It was the ghosts—they were back and still scary-sounding, even in the daytime.

"It's ghosts! She sent them over here

**WHAT THE GHOSTS PROBABLY
LOOK LIKE**

to scare me!" My insides were shaking and I was pulling at Sammy's jacket, which I would not do if things were normal because I would never in a million years touch him on purpose.

"She's mad because of the postcards. Come on! Let's get my dad!" But Sammy was not moving.

"She's not mad. She's got the postcards on her fridge—she likes them. What, do you think she's a witch or something?" Sammy walked away from me and then I heard him yell! I couldn't understand what he was saying. My brain said, "Save Sammy or run for help?" I was running for help when he yelled again, and this time I heard him. He was yelling, "It's Crinkles!"

Crinkles

I ran around the corner of my house, right into Sammy's pointing finger. It was pointing right at me and he said, "You were the catnapper all along! You're a liar!!" Then he pointed at Augustine Dupre's window, which is on my house. Crinkles was looking out at us from inside, and he was making the horrible ghost noises.

~~Forced~~ Partner

It took a long time to tell Sammy Stringer the truth of why Crinkles would be in my house by accident. A normal person would understand the reason really fast, but Sammy Stinger is not a normal person. Plus, he asked me a million hundred questions about every little thing, so the whole story took forever! At the end he believed me that I was not an on-purpose catnapper, which was good, because I was not in a hurry to get into even more trouble. We both looked at Crinkles and we each had our own thoughts, because we did not say anything. My thoughts were . . .

1   I cannot let Dad know where Crinkles is.

2 I must get Crinkles out of Augustine Dupre's apartment.

3 I only want to be grounded for a week . . . not longer, even if things go really, really bad.

I do not know what Sammy Stringer's thoughts were, but I bet they were not as many or as hard as mine.

I had to trade promises with Sammy Stringer so that we could both, in the end, get the thing we wanted. It made us real partners instead of pretend partners like before, which was not so perfect if I thought about who I was a partner with, but much better than being alone if I thought about what I had to do next—it is not easy to be sneaky and careful at the same time if you are all alone.

I tried to open the window, but the little latch thing had snapped closed and the window would not open even a sliver. Sammy said he would stay by the window and talk nice to Crinkles to keep him from howling while I did the sneaking-upstairs part to borrow the spare apartment key from Dad's desk. Sammy also had the job of keeping everyone away from the window in case someone was nosy and came too close. I was not sure if he could do these two things at the same time, but I had to trust him.

Finding the exact key was not easy, because Dad keeps his entire key collection all together in one box and none of the keys has any writing on it to say what it is for. I had to take the whole box outside to Augustine Dupre's door and try almost every single one in the door.

Sammy was nervous that Crinkles would jump through the door the minute I put the right key in, like he was an attack lion or something. If I liked talking to him I would have said, "Don't you think it's crazy to be scared of a cat when you think lions are so great?" but I didn't say that. I said, "He won't jump out. He's just a furry little cozy kittie."

I don't know if Sammy could tell, but

what I said was a little bit mean, but then, because I am not good at being mean, even if someone sort of deserves it like he does, I gave him the two oven mitts I brought down from upstairs so he could protect himself. Sammy seemed a lot happier even though he looked completely silly.

Crinkles was crazy with joy when I opened the door. I told Sammy to stand guard outside until I locked Crinkles in the bathroom, which was not so easy to do because he kept sneaking out when I tried to push him in—plus, his claws were sharp and pointy.

Finally Crinkles was locked up so I could let Sammy in. "It stinks in here! Like a cat bathroom!" said Sammy. He made a really good disgusted face and was trying to hold his nose closed with the big oven mitties.

He was right! It smelled terrible! This whole time while he was locked in, Crinkles was using Augustine Dupre's two fancy trees in pots as a cat toilet.

"Yuck! It's disgusting! It's coming from there," I said, and I pointed at the plants. I 100 percent did not want to touch the smelly pots filled with Crinkles's cat poop, even though I liked Crinkles and he is a very nice cat.

"I'll do it. I'll take them outside," said Sammy. "It's fair, because you have to do the carry-the-cat part." And then right there, even though I could hardly believe it, Sammy turned into the exact perfect-for-me partner. I hate poop and I love cats, and he hates cats and he loves poop. The chance of this per-

fect-partner-happening was probably something like .008 percent.

While Sammy was outside I looked for
some kind of perfumey stuff to spray around
the apartment. Augustine Dupre is fancy, so
she had lots of choices. I used a little bit of
each one, and pretty soon I couldn't even tell
if the cat smell was there anymore.

Sammy said he wanted to wait outside
the apartment when I went upstairs to take
back the keys and the oven mitts. I don't
think he wanted to be in the apartment alone
with Crinkles, but he said it was because he
didn't like the smell of the fancy perfumes.

Cat Return

Sammy walked in front of me and Crinkles just in case Crinkles got away. If Crinkles escaped me, which he was not going to do because I know how to hold a cat, Sammy thought Crinkles would run back to my house instead of in front to Mrs. Luther's house, and he did not want to be a person who was in Crinkles's way. This was perfect with me, because I did not want to be the first person Mrs. Luther saw when she opened her front door.

This was not a problem, because even though Sammy was standing in front, the first thing Mrs. Luther saw was Crinkles. She told me to hold him tight and come in quick so she could close the door so he couldn't run off. Then she asked us to go into the scary mask room and sit down.

I gave her Crinkles and he sat on Mrs. Luther's lap, giving her leg a massage with his claws. This is something cats do when they are happy, and she didn't seem to mind that his claws were sharp and pointy. Mrs. Luther wiped some probably happy tears away from her eyes and said, "So where did you find him?"

I could not believe that Sammy and I had forgotten all about practicing this part.

"Under some bushes near Grace's house."

Yeah, Sammy! He remembered his promise, and he didn't even call me Just Grace like normal.

"Well, thank you, Grace, and thank you, Sammy, for everything." And then Mrs. Luther winked at me and her smile didn't look exactly so much like a crocodile's.

"Sammy, run into the kitchen and get some cookies for you and your friend. He loves my cookies, that Sammy," said Mrs. Luther, and she smiled again—definitely not crocodile-like this time either.

Sammy was right. Mrs. Luther's cookies were amazing. They had real pieces of chocolate bar right in the cookies, which was such a great idea and one I had never seen or eaten before. The masks on the wall still looked kind of scary even up close, but they did not look scarier than they did from my room, which was not how I thought it was going to be. And there was my room, right through Mrs. Luther's window. She could see

COOKIES

REAL
CHOCOLATE
BARS

me as well as I could see her. This was not
something I had thought about either.

MY BEDROOM WINDOW

After the cookies—I got to eat three,
which is a lot of cookies to eat at once if they
are big ones—it was time to go home. Mrs.
Luther locked Crinkles in the kitchen with
some food, then came with Sammy and me
to the door.

Sammy was holding his jar of lion poop
and was so happy, he couldn't stop smiling.
Mrs. Luther had a new kind of cast that she

could walk on, and it was not bright orange.

"Green, my favorite color," she said, pointing at her cast. "Like spring. How about you?"

"Brown," said Sammy. I was thinking it was probably because of poop, but Sammy said, "Like chocolate."

Then it was my turn: "Green, like tree leaves." I couldn't believe that Mrs. Luther and I had the same favorite color and for almost the same exact reason.

"Thank you both so much. I'm glad that you and Sammy are friends!"

"We're not friends," said Sammy, and he smiled at me and I could see bits of chocolate cookie stuck in between his teeth.

I said, "He's right, we're not," and I smiled back at him. But Mrs. Luther had closed her door so she could not hear us anyway.

Then Sammy walked home and I walked home and I thought, *Maybe he's got magnetic teeth. Maybe that's why food gets stuck there.* And I don't know why, but that made it seem a lot less disgusting.

WHAT GRACE WILL BE THINKING ABOUT IN HER NEXT BOOK